LOOKING
for Bear

www.holly-webb.com

LOOKING
for Bear

HOLLY WEBB
Illustrated by Helen Stephens

■SCHOLASTIC

First published in the UK in 2013 by Scholastic Children's Books
An imprint of Scholastic Ltd
Euston House, 24 Eversholt Street
London, NW1 1DB, UK
Registered office: Westfield Road, Southam, Warwickshire, CV47 0RA
SCHOLASTIC and associated logos are trademarks and/
or registered trademarks of Scholastic Inc.

ISBN 978 1 407 13178 8

A CIP catalogue record for this book is
available from the British Library.

Printed and bound by CPI Group (UK) Ltd, Croydon, CR0 44YY
Papers used by Scholastic Children's Books are made
from wood grown in sustainable forests.

1 3 5 7 9 10 8 6 4 2

www.scholastic.co.uk/zone
www.holly-webb.com

For Byron

And for Robin and William,

who first found the bear trap,

and met the pirate builders

1

"When are they coming?" Ben asked, stirring his cereal and watching the milk swirl chocolatey.

"Today! You know it's today." Dad looked round from the toaster. He had that early-morning look, with his hair standing up a bit and his face all creased. "I did tell you."

"Mmmm." Ben ate a couple of spoonfuls. "How many will there be?"

Dad caught the toast as it popped up, and yelped, and then threw it on to Cassie's plate, shaking his fingers.

"It always comes out hot," Cassie told him,

shaking her head. "Silly Daddy."

"Watch it, or I'll eat it for you." Dad sat down between them, smiling. "You know, Ben, I'm not absolutely sure. I think just the two of them. I met them both, when they came to see the house. They're very nice."

Everyone jumped as the doorbell rang. They hadn't lived in the new house all that long, and the bell was particularly loud, like an alarm clock. It surprised them every time.

"They're keen." Dad let out a whistle of surprise. "I didn't think they'd arrive before school. Still, that's good."

He got up and hurried down the hall to the door. Ben and Cassie looked at each other for a second, and then abandoned breakfast and rushed after him.

The builders were standing outside the front door, but with Dad in the way, it was hard to see what they were really like. Ben and Cassie tripped each other up trying to peer round Dad, but they only caught a glimpse of two men grinning at them, and a truck parked out in the street.

"Have you brought a cement mixer?" Cassie demanded, hanging on to Dad's trousers and leaning out of the door. Ben stared at her. She was never shy. He wished he could ask people things like that, without worrying about what to say.

"Not today. But we will, I promise." The man sounded as though he was laughing.

"Good." Cassie nodded, and disappeared back to finish her toast.

As they walked to school, Ben wondered what the house would look like when they got home. The builders had been unloading tools when they hurried out of the house, after a frantic last-minute hunt for Cassie's reading book. The same hunt happened almost every day, and Ben usually found it for her. It had been in her washing basket this morning, and Ben thought she ought to have been a bit more worried about it. But she had raced madly down to the corner just as she always did.

Ben was excited about having a new bedroom – he didn't mind sharing with Cassie that much, but she did leave stuff everywhere. It made it hard for his friends to come round, if they had to climb over Cassie's bears to get to his Lego. And she kept borrowing the Lego too, which was extremely annoying.

If he had his own bedroom, Ben could build the most enormous Lego space station that went up and down his bookshelves, and he wouldn't go to the loo and come back and find a small bear sitting in it.

But it was still weird thinking about the house changing. Even though they'd only lived in it for three months, since just before the summer holidays, Ben really loved it. Mostly because of the garden. It was massive compared to the one at their last house. It had a long, thin lawn (which usually needed cutting, and had quite a lot of toys half-hidden in it), and a patio that was big enough for a table and chairs. Further down the garden, opposite each other, were a greenhouse and a shed, both full of lots of interesting things left by the previous owners. Ben had persuaded Dad to keep the cracked pots for a while, in case something exciting turned out to be growing in them, but there wasn't. There were loads of fat, stripy snails, though.

In the summer holidays, they'd eaten outside a lot. Sometimes breakfast, still in their pyjamas. Even the most boring cereal (the chocolatey ones never lasted very long in Ben and Cassie's house) tasted better outside.

From the house, the garden didn't look as big as it really was, because the end of it was full of trees. It was like having a wood of their very own, and it was one of Ben's favourite things about his new home. It was fantastic for playing hide-and-seek, and there were all sorts of interesting holes where he was sure things were living. Most of the trees were big old ones that were a bit too tall to climb still, but Ben wasn't giving up. Once he'd worked out how to get up the trees, he was going to build a tree house, and take Dad's binoculars up there with him. His grandpa had taken him bird-watching, but Ben had found it a bit slow. He was planning something more exciting. It would be better to watch for badgers, or squirrels, or maybe even bears. The trees were definitely big enough for bears to lurk behind. He liked the thought of stretching out on a platform, high in the trees, spying on the bears as they lumbered past. He'd have a sketchbook, too, and draw their portraits.

The trees towered over the greenhouse, which was still a bit battered and spidery, but full of plants now. Dad had taken them to the garden centre, and they'd bought some tomato plants, and pumpkins, because Cassie wanted to grow one for Halloween. The tomatoes had shot up to the glass roof, and the pumpkin plants were like some sort of vegetable-y alien. They had grown all round the inside of the greenhouse, armed with tangly little coils that attached themselves to anything. There was actually a pumpkin, but it was only big enough to fit a birthday candle in. Cassie sang to it, a silly song about spooky castles that she'd learned in Reception. Over and over and over. She said it was to encourage it to get bigger in time.

Dad wanted to do all sorts of things to the garden, but he was too busy with work – he was an accountant, which basically meant he sorted out other people's money for them.

Occasionally very worried-looking people came for meetings in Dad's office (which would have been the biggest bedroom, in most houses) carrying large plastic bags full of bits of paper, which they would give Ben's dad with apologetic looks on their faces. Being a very good accountant (who never told anybody off about the bits of paper) meant that Dad was working all the time that Ben and Cassie were at school, and even when they were in bed. And Ben was pretty sure he was thinking about work a lot of the rest of the time as well, when he was cooking the dinner, or doing the vacuuming.

It made him quite hard to play with

sometimes. Dad was actually very good at Lego, and excellent at computer games. He could join in with dressing up Cassie's bears, if she told him exactly what to do. But he didn't often have time, and even when they did make him play (Cassie was very good at ambushing him with a dressing-up costume, so he didn't have a choice) he never lasted long before he had to go and answer an email, or call someone at once. Ben had tried to draw him, sometimes, too, but Dad never sat still long enough for Ben to finish a picture.

Cassie skipped back down the pavement towards Ben and Dad. "Will the house still be all there when we get home?"

Dad grinned. "They aren't knocking any of it down, Cass!"

"Aren't they?" Cassie sounded disappointed.

"Well, they'll have to knock a hole through for the staircase. But not until the loft's nearly ready. Until then they'll just go up and down the scaffolding."

"Knock a hole *in the floor*?" Ben asked, amazed. It sounded a bit – drastic. A bit dangerous. "What if the whole house falls down?"

"Will it?" Cassie asked excitedly. "It isn't that I want it to," she added quickly. "But if all my bears got squashed, I could have new ones."

"More bears!" Ben rolled his eyes, and Cassie drew in a breath to tell him off.

"You'll have to choose what colour you want your rooms painted," Dad put in hurriedly, before Cassie and Ben could start fighting.

Cassie's eyes widened. "Any colour?" she said at last, hopefully. "Pink? With stripes?"

"Er… We'll think about it…"

"Could I paint mine myself?" Ben asked, staring pleadingly at Dad. "I mean, I'd paint it all white, and then I could draw on it?"

He half-closed his eyes, seeing pictures behind his eyelids, spread out all over the white walls of a whole room. It would be brilliant – and then, when he'd covered it all, he could just get some more white paint and start all over again.

Ben frowned. Actually, though, what if he wanted to keep any of the stuff he had drawn? Perhaps he'd be able to just paint over bits of it.

"I've never had a stripy bedroom," Cassie was twittering to Dad beside him. "Or maybe

I could have it all covered in flowers? And a bear asleep in them? Can I have a blue ceiling with clouds on it?"

Ben thought Dad looked quite relieved once they got to school and Cassie disappeared into the heaving mass in the playground.

"The house will be all right, won't it?" he asked Dad as they stood waiting for the bell to ring.

"It will. It'll be fine. I'll be there to make sure, Ben." Dad gave him a quick one-armed hug. "You can come back and see what they've done this afternoon."

2

Ben was usually one of the last people in his class to get out into the playground after school. There always seemed to be something he had to find, like his water bottle, or his jumper. But today he stuffed everything into his backpack and raced out.

"Ben! Ben!" Cassie was standing with Dad, jumping up and down and waving to him. "Come on! The builders will leave at five, Dad says. We haven't got much time to see what they're doing."

"But remember, you mustn't get in their way," Dad warned her. "Hey, Ben. Want me to take anything?"

Ben handed Dad his coat and they set off, with Cassie buzzing round Ben and Dad like an agitated fly. "We should have brought our scooters, it would have been faster. Walk quicker, Ben!"

Cassie ran ahead of them all the way up the road, darting in and out of the other families walking home and then suddenly appearing like a little fair-haired terrier in front of them, panting crossly.

"Wow," Ben gasped as they came round the corner of their road. He was a good bit taller than Cassie, and he could see the house when she couldn't.

"What is it? What is it? Are you teasing me? Oooh!" Cassie stopped and stared at the scaffolding that had grown up the side wall of the house since they'd been gone, like some strange, silvery creeper.

Ben looked at it thoughtfully. "Are we allowed to—"

"No!" his dad said quickly. "Absolutely not. Ever. In fact, I had to promise the builders solemnly that you wouldn't."

"It looks like the climbing frame in the playground," Cassie argued as they reached the house and stood looking up at the scaffolding.

"But it's twice as tall," Dad began to explain, when another voice broke in.

"And if you fall off it, you'll fall on the concrete path, or the patio. And I'm not scraping you up like strawberry jam. Not in my contract."

The voice came from up above them. There was a flapping tarpaulin thrown over one of the scaffolding bars, and they hadn't seen that there was someone behind it on a wooden platform. Now he leaned over the bars to look at them, and they eyed him cautiously.

"Exactly," Dad said, his eyes crinkling at the corners. "So no. This is Dave, and he's in charge. You need to listen to him, all right? And Les."

Another man came walking along the wooden platform that ran round from the back of the house, with a big mug in his hand.

Cassie drew in her breath with an excited gasp as soon as she saw him, and Ben knew why. Les had long, greyish hair, a grey beard and a gold earring in one ear. He was wearing a baseball cap on backwards, but if he'd changed it for a spotted bandanna tied over his head, he would have looked exactly like a pirate.

He waved, and called, "Hey, you two." But Ben was too shy to say anything back, and Cassie was awestruck. They scuttled into the house, dumping their coats and bags, and then Cassie tugged Ben into the living room.

"He's a pirate!" she whispered frantically as soon as she'd shut the door.

"No, he isn't," Ben told her, in the special older-brother voice he kept just for times like this. "Don't be silly. Pirates are only in books."

"No!" Cassie shook her head firmly. "They used to be real, didn't they? They're history."

"The thing about history is that it doesn't happen any more!" Ben said, rolling his eyes. "That's because it's *history*, Cass. Really old. Ancient. There aren't any pirates now."

"He looks like a pirate." Cassie marched over to the door and glared at Ben. "He's got an earring. And his hair's right. He definitely is. I'll prove it."

Ben followed her as she trotted back into the hall. The carpet was covered in a strange sort of sticky stuff, like the sticky-backed plastic they were supposed to put over their homework books now that they were in Year Three. There was so much fuss now. Sometimes he wished he was back in the Infants, like Cassie. She was only a year younger than he was, but no one ever seemed to tell her off about anything.

"Where are you going?" he called after her.

Cassie didn't bother answering; she just thundered up the stairs to their bedroom, and Ben hurried behind her.

"Do you want a snack?" Dad called from the kitchen, but neither of them answered.

"Look, I thought so." Cassie leaned on their bedroom windowsill. "The scaffolding comes round the side of the house."

"So what? The window looks out at the garden," Ben objected. "We won't be able to see them."

"But we can listen," Cassie whispered dramatically. "We can see if they talk about pirate things."

Ben snorted with laughter. "Like where to buy the best parrots?"

Cassie shook her head and sighed. "You'll see. Just because you didn't think of it." She opened the window a little, and then stationed herself determinedly on the end of her bed, kneeling up with her elbows on the windowsill and her chin on her hands.

Ben shook his head and settled down on the floor, drawing a house with scaffolding in the biggest of his drawing pads. It was his favourite one, with the wire spiral binding and the fat paper. He only got it out for the best drawings. He smiled to himself as he flicked through to a clean page. The last drawing he'd done was one of Cassie, playing hide-and-seek in the trees at the end of the garden. He'd added a bear creeping up behind her.

There were faint noises coming from out on the scaffolding. Clangings and mutters. And someone humming. But no discussion of treasure, or the high seas. Cassie began to droop a little, and eventually, with a shifty look at Ben, she wriggled off the end of her bed and started to play with her family of tiny bears.

Ben considered teasing her, but didn't. Even if he didn't believe there were such things as pirates these days, it would have been very cool to have a pirate building his bedroom. He was almost a little bit disappointed too.

The humming floated through the window, and then changed to whistling – a tune Ben thought he knew – and then a few of the words:

"What shall we do with the drunken sailor? What shall we do with the drunken sailor? What shall we do with the drunken sailor, ear-ly in the morning?"

Ben and Cassie looked at each other for a second, wide-eyed, and then they scrambled up to get to the window.

"I told you so!" said Cassie, her eyes sparkling excitedly.

"It doesn't mean he's a pirate," Ben said, gripping the windowsill tightly as they craned their necks to try and see round the side of the house.

"It's a pirate song!" Cassie glared at him.

"Why would a pirate be working on our house?" Ben pointed out. "We don't even live near the sea."

Cassie wrinkled her nose thoughtfully. "Maybe he's retired. Or his ship sank! If he didn't have enough treasure, he might have had to get another job."

Ben shrugged. That did sort of make sense, and there was no point arguing with Cassie sometimes. She was just never going to listen.

3

Ben mooched around the playground at break, thinking to himself. The builders had arrived just as they had left for school that morning. They had been standing in front of the garage door, drinking mugs of tea. They'd waved to Ben and Cassie, and the children had waved shyly back. Cassie didn't usually have any trouble talking to people, but she wasn't sure how to ask Les if he was actually a pirate. It was making her silent. She just stared at him instead, with wide, fascinated eyes.

She had elbowed Ben hard as they went past them. "Stripy socks!" she hissed to Ben, as they followed Dad out on to the pavement.

"Dad has stripy socks, you know. And I do. So do you!"

Cassie flounced off after Dad. She seemed to think that Ben was being deliberately difficult, but he wasn't really. He didn't want her to get all excited and then find out the truth and be miserable. Like when she discovered that the fairy princess who did storytime at the library was actually Miss Atkins the librarian dressed up. She had refused to ever go back.

Suddenly he flinched as a football flew past his ear, and he watched it bounce away towards the fence.

"Kick it back, Ben!" yelled his friend Sam, from the other side of the playground.

Ben booted it towards them, but he wasn't really concentrating, and the ball shot sideways and landed in a group of girls who were doing a complicated skipping game.

"Hey!" one of them, a girl from the year above, shouted. She glared at him and kicked the ball back, hard, and much more accurately than he had.

It hit Ben in the stomach, leaving him panting. He hadn't fallen over but he looked silly, standing there with his eyes all round and his breath coming in little gasps.

Everyone laughed, and Ben went slowly red, a dark, purplish flush that burned across his cheeks.

"Are you all right?" Sam came over and picked up the ball. He looked embarrassed.

Ben nodded. "Yes," he said huskily. "I just missed – I didn't mean to kick it into those girls."

They were still laughing. He could see them giggling, and talking to each other behind their hands. The one who'd kicked the ball looked triumphant, and faintly nervous at the same time, in case he told.

Sam sighed. "Come on. Come and play with us."

Ben nodded. He quite liked playing football. He just hadn't felt like it earlier; he'd been too busy thinking about the builders. He followed Sam back towards the group of boys, who were watching impatiently.

Somehow, it wasn't a good game. No one passed to him very much, and he tripped over

James and scraped the side of his leg. James didn't even say sorry properly, he just rolled his eyes and mumbled something.

Even Sam glared at him when he accidentally scored a goal in between the wrong pair of school jumpers. Ben was quite glad when the bell rang.

Some of the boys in his class kept glancing over at him during literacy. James's friend Kurt, and Leo, who was always telling people that his dad used to be a professional footballer, sat on the other side of Ben and Sam's table. They kept looking at him, and then at each other, and whispering stuff behind their hands.

Ben was certain they were all talking about him, and how rubbish he was. It was very hard to concentrate on the comprehension work they were supposed to be doing. He wanted to ask Sam what was going on, but something stopped him. Sam wasn't whispering with the others, but he didn't seem to be talking much to Ben either. Sam just kept looking down at his work – not muttering jokes in Ben's ear or complaining about how mean Mrs Pearce was, like he usually did.

Ben's class were on the second sitting for lunch, so they went straight out into the playground, the boys racing ahead. Kurt and Leo and James spilled out into the grassy area, squabbling over a football. As the others came up, James snatched it and glared around. He usually ended up in charge of the lunch-time games – just because he was big, and loud, and nobody really liked arguing with him. And he was very, very good at football. He played for a proper team, and he always seemed to have his picture in the local paper that came through the door.

"You're on my team," he told Leo, and elbowed Kurt. "You can pick the other team."

Kurt folded his arms and stared at the ten or so boys crowding around them. Ben hung back, thinking he'd probably get picked last, and not wanting to look as though he minded.

James and Kurt squabbled their way through picking the teams, until everyone but Ben had been chosen. Ben shifted from foot to foot, and wondered if he should say anything. Remind them he was there, perhaps? Maybe it was just that he was standing behind Sam. Except now he wasn't, because James had picked Sam almost first.

"Ummm…" he murmured, waving a hand shyly. "Um, whose team can I go on?"

James and Kurt exchanged glances. "You can't," James said flatly. "You're not good enough to play."

Ben gasped. It felt like being hit with that football all over again. He could hardly get the words out. "But – but—" he stuttered, and the other boys smirked.

"You're useless," Kurt added. "We don't want you in our game." He sniggered. "Even those girls are better than you."

"Hey…" Sam murmured, staring at the ground. But that was all he said, even when

Ben looked at him beseechingly. He'd always thought Sam would stand up for him. He would have done, if someone had said something like that to Sam. In fact, he had, back at the beginning of the year, when Sam couldn't get his head round fractions. James and the others had been laughing at him and calling him thick because he had to stay in at lunch for extra lessons with Mrs Pearce. Usually Ben wasn't very good at thinking up quick answers, but Sam had been almost crying, and it had made Ben furious. He'd told James to shut his face, and who cared about fractions anyway? James had been so surprised that he actually had shut up, although it didn't last for long. But it had given Sam time to feel better, which was what mattered.

"Get lost, Ben," James said. Ben could tell that he was really enjoying himself. "You're in the way."

Ben gave one last look at Sam, but Sam was still ignoring him. He wouldn't even look up. So Ben walked away, like he'd been told to. It was hard even to do that. He felt so upset that his legs were shaking.

Ben walked over to the wall at the edge of the playground and leaned against it, trying to look as though that was what he really wanted to be doing. What he actually  wanted to do was cry, but he wasn't going to give James and Kurt the satisfaction. It was hard not to, though. The crying was balled in the middle of him, sitting in his throat, and it seemed to be getting bigger and bigger.

He sniffed, loudly and defiantly, and looked round for someone else to go and play with.

The problem was that all the boys in his class were playing football – every single one of them. Ben was quite friendly with some of the girls, but not enough that he could just walk up to a gang of them and join in with whatever they were doing. So as not to look as if he had nothing to do, Ben walked briskly round the edge of the playground, hoping to find someone he could hang around with. And so he could get far enough away from the football game to blow his nose. He really didn't want the almost-crying to be obvious.

"Hey, Ben!" Cassie chirped as she raced past him with one of the other girls from her class dashing after her. Tag – he wasn't bad at that. He wasn't the world's fastest runner, but he was OK.

Ben almost yelled after her, to ask if he could play, but then he stopped himself.

Playing with his little sister? Who was still in the Infants? And all her little girl friends? He could just imagine how James would make it sound. *Ahhhh, little baby Benny. Playing with the little girls. Why don't you wear one of your little sister's dresses tomorrow, Ben?*

He couldn't.

"Are you all right, Ben?" Mrs Pearce was on playground duty, and she actually sounded quite nice. She was a lot stricter than any of the teachers they'd had before, and she made a huge fuss about work being neat and homework getting handed in on time. But sometimes she was fun – she liked art, like Ben did, and she always admired his pictures.

"I'm OK," he muttered.

"Not playing football?" Mrs Pearce asked,

gazing thoughtfully across the playground at the other boys.

Ben shrugged. "Didn't feel like it."

"Mmmm."

He had a feeling that Mrs Pearce knew exactly why he wasn't playing football, and she didn't like it much.

"Do you want to go and help Mrs Lake with the cutting out for this afternoon?" Mrs Pearce suggested, and he glanced up at her in grateful surprise. "It won't be all that exciting, but I bet she'd like a hand. Tell her I sent you."

Ben nodded and hurried off inside. It was a lucky rescue, and he knew it. But he couldn't spend the rest of the week's lunch times lurking in the classroom with the teachers.

★

"Dad…"

"Mmm?" Dad didn't sound as though he was properly paying attention. He was frowning, and Ben guessed he'd been in the middle of something for work before he came out to fetch them from school.

"Do you think you could teach me to play football better? This weekend, maybe? Tomorrow?"

Dad blinked. "I didn't think you were all that keen on football."

Ben shrugged. "I like watching it. But I'm no good at playing."

"Don't worry about it, Ben. It doesn't matter if you're not great at football. You can still have a lot of fun kicking a ball around anyway. You're better at swimming. And running; you're a good runner. I'd stick to those if I were you."

"Yes, but…" It was hard to describe what had happened at lunch time – for a start because Ben still really didn't want to talk about it. It was making him want to cry even now, all this time later.

"What are you talking about?" Cassie had suddenly darted back to them from further up the road, where she'd been walking with her friend Maia.

"Nothing," Ben said, flushing scarlet again. It was bad enough Cassie having millions of friends and never being shy and being good at practically everything while he felt useless, without her actually knowing about it as well.

Dad looked down at him, as though he'd finally noticed something wasn't right. "You OK, Ben? Was it not a good day?"

Ben shook his head. Not with Cassie listening. "Just boring. I'm fine. What's for tea?"

4

"They've dug a massive great big hole in the garden!" Ben said to Cassie, turning round from the window. "Look!" He'd changed out of his uniform into a T-shirt and jeans – it was still really hot, even though it was the end of September. He'd happened to look out at the garden as he dragged the T-shirt over his head.

Cassie came over and looked out. "What's that for?" she said, gazing at it. "Why do they need a hole?" She gave a little gasp and grabbed his arm. "Maybe they're burying treasure! I *knew* they were pirates."

Ben shrugged. He was still sure she was wrong, but he just didn't feel like arguing. Being miserable was very tiring.

"Let's go and ask them." Cassie hurried out of the door. He could hear her thundering down the stairs, calling, "Les! Les!"

The builders were packing their tools away – they were storing some of them in the shed at the bottom of Ben and Cassie's garden. Dave was pushing a heavy wheelbarrow up the garden while Les stacked things away.

Ben stopped by the hole, staring into it and wondering what on earth it was really for. Cassie hurried across the grass, shouting to the builders.

"What's the big hole for? Are you burying treasure? Have you got lots? Are you going to leave it here? Will you make a map so you don't forget where to come and dig it up?"

Ben saw Dave and Les exchange a grin as they locked up the shed and walked back towards the hole, with Cassie skipping backwards before them.

Dave shook his head thoughtfully. "No, that's not where we're burying our treasure."

Cassie glared triumphantly at Ben – so they did have some! "What's the hole for then? Please can you tell us? It *is* our garden!"

Dave nodded slowly, importantly. "Good point. You probably ought to know anyway, so you're sure to stay away from it."

"Definitely," Les agreed.

"What is it?" Cassie begged.

"It's a bear trap."

Ben and Cassie gaped at Les. Ben had been expecting the builders to tease them with some sort of pirate story – he was pretty sure that Les had heard what Cassie was saying about him and had sung that sea shanty on purpose. He was enjoying being a pirate.

Ben certainly hadn't expected bears.

Cassie was enchanted. Bears were even better than pirates. Didn't she have seventeen of them lined up along her bed? "A bear trap for bears?" she whispered.

"A bear trap for bears," Dave agreed solemnly. "See you on Monday then," he added. "We're off home now."

"You can't go!" Cassie shrieked. "You have to tell us about the bears! What sort of bears is it for? Big ones? Do they come in our garden?

Will we see them?" She frowned. "What if one gets in the trap this weekend when you're not here? What do we do with it?"

"Feed it some sausage rolls," Les told her. "Everyone thinks bears like honey, but actually, what they really want is a nice sausage roll." He looked at the hole thoughtfully. "Maybe you're right. Perhaps we'll cover it up, just for the weekend. So you don't get stuck with a hungry bear." He went over to fetch a piece of board that had been leaning up against the fence.

Ben was peering into the hole. It didn't really look deep enough for a bear. Not a big one, anyway. A small bear might fall in it and not be able to climb out... He shook his head crossly. It was all made up anyway. The builders were just teasing Cassie. He was far too big to be taken in by stupid stories.

Dave grinned at him. "Don't believe me, do you?" he asked as he helped Les lay the board over the hole.

Ben shook his head and frowned. "No." He'd imagined bears in the garden, but that's all it was. Imagining.

"Oh, Ben!" Cassie sounded horrified.

Dave shrugged. "You will. You'll see one, one of these days. You just keep an eye on those trees at the bottom of your garden. Full of bears, they are."

From then on, Cassie watched the garden for bears, spending hours perched on the bedroom windowsill, staring out at the trees.

She told all her friends at school, and they believed her – so much so that Maia begged and begged to be allowed to sleep over and watch for bears too. Cassie and Maia almost stopped being friends when Cassie said that they were her bears, and she had to see one first. Maia even came and asked Ben if it was true and whether he really did have bears in his garden.

Every morning when Cassie got up, she ran downstairs in her pyjamas to check the bear trap, but they'd never caught one.

"Clever bears, yours," Dave said, shrugging, when she asked him about it. "Too clever to be caught. Maybe you ought to bait the trap if you really want to catch one."

Cassie reported this to Ben. She knew he

didn't believe in the bears, but she needed him to help. She didn't like sausage rolls, and Dad knew that perfectly well. So she couldn't go asking him to buy any – even if he believed that she'd started liking them, then he'd expect her to eat them.

"It took ages to make him remember I hate sausage rolls," she told Ben. "I'm not having them in my packed lunch for years and years. I just want them for the bear trap. So will you ask him to get some when we go shopping? Please?"

"How are you going to explain it when they've all gone from the fridge?" Ben asked.

Cassie smiled persuasively at him. "We'll just tell Dad you ate them. Please, Ben? I'll give you two of my mint humbugs."

Ben thought she'd forget that the next time she got sweets, but he agreed anyway. Officially, he didn't believe in the bear story. But there was something about the way Cassie watched so faithfully, sitting on the windowsill every evening as the garden darkened and the shadows spilled out from the trees, bringing the possibility of bears with them… It made Ben want to catch one too.

It was the night they baited the trap that Cassie saw one – or she said she did. Ben was falling asleep, listening to Dad tapping away on the computer in the next room. Cassie was supposed to be in bed as well – Dad had already read them a story, and the lights were out. But she'd sneaked out of bed to watch for bears again, sure that tonight the sausage rolls would tempt the bears closer to the house. She'd laid a trail, leading right up to the trap.

Cassie's scream brought Ben awake again in a split second. He sat up in bed, gasping.

Cassie was kneeling right up on the windowsill, her hands pressed flat against the glass. "I saw one! I saw one! I really did! Oh, look, he's running away, he must have heard me."

Dad opened the bedroom door and came in looking worried. "What happened? Did you have a bad dream? Cassie, what are you doing on the windowsill?"

"I saw a bear! It was eating the sausage rolls, Dad. I knew it would."

Dad picked her up and cuddled her. "Just a dream, sweetheart. Get back into bed, it's late."

"Oh, but I want to see him again…" Cassie murmured as Dad wrapped her duvet round her. But she was almost asleep, Ben could hear it in her voice. Perhaps she'd been asleep all the time – Dad obviously thought so.

She must have dreamed the bear…

"So what did it look like?" Ben asked her, scuffing through a pile of leaves as they walked along under the trees in the park. Dad had finished a big job, and suggested an afternoon out. He said he was sorry he'd been so busy, and that they deserved lunch at the café by the canal. They loved walking along there – the canal ran along one side of the park, and there were always boats moored there.

"Big," said Cassie slowly. They hadn't had much time to talk about the bear without Dad around, but now he'd bumped into someone whose accounts he did, and had stopped to chat. "It was just – big."

"Is that all?" Ben said disappointedly.

"It was dark! I couldn't see much. It was big, and slow. Until it ran away when I screamed. It was quite fast then."

"I bet it wasn't a bear. It was probably the cat from next door."

"It was not! It was much bigger than that. Loads bigger. And furrier. A cat!" She rolled her eyes disgustedly.

"Don't go too near the water!" Dad called, catching them up. "Wow, lots of boats moored up today."

They all loved looking at the boats. Cassie liked the painted decorations, and reading the names, but Ben always imagined living on one. Particularly now. If you woke up in a different bit of river every morning, how could you possibly go to school? Break times were getting worse. He still wasn't allowed to play football, and James and Kurt had started to say he was useless at whatever game they played. He wasn't often allowed to join in. Sometimes Sam pulled him into a game without anyone saying anything, but mostly Ben just had to watch.

He shook his head, hurrying closer to the

boats and refusing to allow school to spoil the weekend too. He loved the way they moved so slowly, sauntering gently between the banks, getting overtaken by the ducks. There was time to watch things. No hurrying.

"Oh, look at this one…" Cassie called back to him. "It's called *Midnight*. Look at the stars. It's like a pirate boat. The sort of boat a pirate would live on when he'd retired from proper pirating."

The boat was black, with her name in silver and gold paint. Most of the other canal boats had flowers painted on them, roses and bright patterns. But this one was decorated with silver stars swirling around her name and scattering out down the sides of the boat.

"I wonder who lives on it," Ben murmured.

He was quite sure it wasn't just a holiday boat, as some of them were. There was a cat on it, for a start. A fat black one to match the paintwork, with a spotted handkerchief tied round its neck for a collar. It was sitting on the roof of the boat, in the middle of a coil of rope, gazing down at the children with round green eyes and a superior expression.

"Oh, I wish we could stroke it," Cassie said, stretching up a hand to the cat, who ignored her. "It's beautiful."

Dad laughed. "Don't talk so loud, Cassie. You'll wake the owner up, look." He pointed to a deckchair, set in the stern of the boat. A man was fast asleep, with a baseball cap pulled down over his eyes. Dad put his finger to his lips. "Come on. Let's go and get some lunch."

Cassie ran after him, waving goodbye to the cat, but Ben lingered, staring at the boat and its owner. Dad and Cassie hadn't seen – they hadn't looked as closely as he had. The man in the deckchair had an earring, and long grey hair, and he'd winked at Ben as Cassie hurried away.

It was Les.

After that, it was much easier to believe that Les was a pirate. A retired pirate, maybe, who'd given up sailing the high seas and hunting treasure for a quieter sort of life. And if Les really was a pirate, then surely the other stories were true too? Which meant there really were bears living at the bottom of Ben and Cassie's garden. Ben had wanted to believe they were there before, but now he was almost convinced.

When they got back home, Ben went out into the garden to search for evidence. If there really were bears living in the little thicket of trees, there had to be proof.

The sausage rolls that Cassie had left as bait the day before had gone, but all sorts of creatures could have taken them. Next door's cat would eat anything, although a whole packet of sausage rolls might have been a bit much. Only a much bigger animal could have eaten them all – and what was bigger than a bear? Ben crouched down, peering at the damp earth. Maybe he could find a paw print. It was good that it had rained last night – tracks wouldn't show on dry soil.

"What are you doing?" Cassie asked, right behind him, and Ben jumped, nearly overbalancing into the flower bed.

"Don't creep up on me like that!" he gasped. "I was looking for prints."

Cassie blinked. "Fingerprints? Why?"

"No..." Ben looked at her sideways. "Paw prints. Bear prints." He shrugged. "All the sausage rolls have gone."

Cassie nodded excitedly. "Yes! The paw prints will be enormous. It was a huge bear, I told you." She knelt down beside him on the grass, peering in between the straggly plants. "I can't see anything," she said at last, in a doubtful sort of voice.

Ben sighed. "No. Me neither. All I've found is ants. And I bet they like sausage rolls too."

Cassie sat down on the grass next to him and patted his shoulder, the way Dad did when Ben was upset. "I think it would take an awful lot of ants to carry a sausage roll," she pointed out seriously. "Even if it didn't leave any footprints, I bet anything it was a bear."

5

"What did you do to your arm?" Ben asked, watching Les shovel sand into the cement mixer after school on Monday. He'd stopped being shy round the builders now. Besides, anyone who lived on a boat like that was worth listening to, Ben thought. He hadn't told Cassie who lived on *Midnight* until they got back home – it was his secret just for a little while. Now, of course, Cassie was absolutely convinced that she'd been right all along, and Les was a pirate. And the cat had been his ship's cat, before he retired.

Les stopped shovelling and looked at the

long scratch. It went from his elbow almost down to his wrist. He shook his head sadly and looked sideways at Cassie. "The parrot bit me."

"You've got a parrot as well?" Cassie squeaked. "Doesn't your cat chase him?"

"He wouldn't dare." Les shook his head. "He's pretty fierce, old Captain. He'd have Sampson's whiskers out, or worse."

Ben grinned. He had one of his drawing pads balanced on his lap – he was sitting on the back step, so as to watch Dave and Les mixing up cement on the patio – and he turned over a new page, blocking it out into squares for a comic strip. He was quite good at drawing cats, but he didn't think he'd ever drawn a parrot – the beak was tricky.

"Oh, that's really good." Cassie leaned over to see. "Look, Les! Ben's drawn your cat, and Captain!"

Les came and stood next to them – he was smiling, but when he looked down at the sketchbook, his face changed from just being nice to really being impressed. "That *is* good," he said admiringly. "Looks just like Sampson. You're really good, Ben. You should look at this, Dave!"

Ben shrugged, but it felt nice to have someone say so.

"Can I see the rest of the book?" Dave asked, crouching down beside him on the step. "You drawn any of us?"

"A couple," Ben admitted, going red, as Dave flicked over the pages. Somehow, Cassie going on and on about pirates had made him want to draw them. When he'd seen Les on *Midnight*, it had seemed so right to come home and draw him on a pirate ship, a black one with starry sails. And then he'd just kept drawing, not really thinking, until the pirate ship lifted off the page and went sailing up into the sky.

"That's a bit silly, that one..." he said, shrugging, as Dave and Les stared at it.

"Not silly at all. You're an artist, Ben."

"You should make a book out of them," Dave said, shaking his head. "All those ideas bursting out of you; you're so lucky."

Ben stared at him. He didn't think he was lucky at all. "No one else thinks they're any good," he muttered. "And they're all I'm any good at."

"Don't your friends at school like your pictures?" Les asked, looking surprised. "I'd have thought they'd all be wanting you to draw them!"

Ben shrugged. "No one thinks drawing's cool. They're all into football, and nothing else matters. They'd say drawing was for girls."

"What's wrong with girls?" Cassie demanded. "Girls are better at *everything*. I hate that boy James in your class. He's stupid, and he's mean. He pushed Claudia over – he just walked past her and pushed her out of his way. He didn't even stop and say sorry! We told Mrs Mason, and she said it was an accident and we were just making a fuss."

Ben sighed. "He never gets in trouble."

Cassie wriggled her arm round Ben's waist. "You're much nicer than all of them. Will you draw me, Ben, please? Me in a pirate costume? A pirate dress?"

Ben was very good at drawing Cassie, because she made him do it so often. He put her in the crow's nest at the top of the mast of a pirate ship, looking out across the sea with a telescope. It was odd, drawing with an audience. Dave and Les were looking over his shoulder, laughing, and talking about his picture. He felt like he was on a stage. It was actually very exciting – although it definitely made it harder than just drawing on his own, curled up on his bed.

"Look at that – you've got the hair exactly right," Dave murmured admiringly. Cassie's hair was curly, and it stuck out everywhere. Ben had drawn it springing out from underneath a big skull-and-crossbones pirate hat, with Cassie frowning at the telescope, the way she always did when she was thinking hard about something.

Ben finished the drawing and held it out for them all to see.

"I'm much nicer looking than that," said Cassie. "But it's quite good."

"I don't suppose you'd sell it, Ben?" Les reached into his pockets. "For fifty pence and a Werther's Original? All I've got on me at the moment…"

Ben flushed scarlet. "You'd really want to buy it?"

"You have to sign it first, though. Ten years'

time when you're famous, I have to be able to prove it's a real Ben Daunt."

Carefully, Ben wrote his name in the corner, then tore the page out and accepted the sweet and the fifty pence. "Thanks. I'm saving up for a new football. My old one's a bit squishy and I've got to practise."

"You practising for a special match, then?" Les asked as he carefully laid the picture on top of the bags of screws in his huge metal toolbox.

Ben shook his head, staring down at his feet. "Not really."

"No one at school lets him play," Cassie called. She was dancing around on the patio with a bottle of bubble mixture, twirling the bubbles round her head. "They said he isn't good enough at football."

Ben felt his face burning, and the blood seemed to rush and swirl suddenly in his ears. He hadn't realized that Cassie had noticed what was going on. She'd never said.

"If I practise I'll get better," he muttered, furiously slapping at a bubble that had come too close.

Les nodded slowly. "That matters, then. You've got to be good?"

"Yes," Ben whispered, suddenly feeling that he never would be. Not like the others. "I have to go and practise," he said sharply, standing up and letting his sketchbook tip off his lap, pages fluttering wildly as it fell in the dust. He ran away from them up the garden, shoving past Cassie and her stupid bubbles. He ignored her furious squeak and dodged round behind the shed, between the fence and the trees. He was half-hoping that Cassie would follow him so he could yell at her, but the other half of him wanted to be left alone. So everyone knew! Even people in the Infants knew that Ben Daunt was useless. He dragged his sleeve across his eyes and gulped.

His football was in the shed somewhere. He peered round the corner and saw that Dave and Les had gone. Cassie had gone with them to say goodbye. She liked standing on the doorstep and waving people off. Ben yanked the shed door open, looking at the tangled mess of stuff inside. All the garden tools and lots of random junk had been dumped in here when they moved.

Ben lifted up the saggy paddling pool and

found his football underneath it, with a water pistol and an old Frisbee he'd forgotten about. He picked the football up reluctantly. It wasn't as much fun, kicking the ball about on his own. It would have been better if Sam could have come round and they'd practised together. But neither of them had asked for the other to come round this week. It just hadn't felt right. It would have been too difficult not to talk about what was happening at school, and they certainly didn't want to do that.

Ben walked out on to the grass, his shoulders sagging. He dropped the ball down in front of him and tried to feel excited about improving his football skills. But the ball just sat there in the too-long grass, and he didn't want to play at all. He sat down next to it, cross-legged, and stared at it miserably. He ought to just take a pad and pencils out into the playground and not care if people said drawing was stupid. But he did care. It was too hard.

There was an odd rustling noise from the greenhouse, over on the other side of the narrow garden, which made Ben jump. He could see the pumpkin plants at the back moving. Ben shook himself crossly. No, they weren't. That sounded like one of those horror comics Sam liked. Mutant pumpkins. Alien plants. But now Ben looked closer he saw the plants weren't moving at all. Something was in the greenhouse, shaking the leaves about.

It was probably Cassie. Except Cassie had gone to say goodbye to Dave and Les; she wasn't in the garden.

Ben stood up. He knew one of the big glass panes at the back of the greenhouse was missing – maybe a cat or something had got inside? He stomped firmly over to the greenhouse, thinking that if there was anything in there – a fox? a rat? – his heavy footsteps would scare it away.

It was as Ben pushed open the heavy sliding door that he suddenly realized what it might be. The pumpkin plants had grown all across the back of the greenhouse, like a tiny patch of jungle. A jungle big enough to hide a bear.

There were pale pastry crumbs scattered over the cement floor of the greenhouse,

and the dark, slightly hairy leaves of the pumpkin plants were still shaking.

Stop it, thought Ben. *Don't be silly.* It was only Dave and Les making up stories to tease Cassie. The bears were only as real as the pirates. But now Ben had seen the canalboat, and the ship's cat, and Les's parrot-scratched arm. It had to be true. And there *was* something in his greenhouse. He stood clutching the door and peering at the shivering leaves and wishing it would come out so he could see it, but also hoping that it wouldn't... What if it was huge like Cassie had said?

There was a flurry of movement among the leaves and a scratchy, scraping noise. The greenhouse shook a little, and a dark, gleaming eye looked out at Ben between the leaves. Then he caught a glimpse of golden-brown fur, as something largish hurried away from him to the shelter of the trees.

Ben stared after it.

6

It had to have been a bear. What else could it have been? Ben breathed out. He hadn't even realized he'd been holding his breath.

Dave and Les had been right. His own bear... A bear who lived in the greenhouse. It made sense now he thought about it. It would be much warmer sleeping in there than outside on the ground, or in a cave. Actually, Ben couldn't think of any caves close to where they lived. And none of the trees at the end of the garden were hollow enough to house a bear.

And of course it would have just picked up the sausage rolls and gone back to its den. It probably curled up under those huge leaves – or on the bag of compost; it was softish, a little bit cushiony. It wouldn't have been at all interested in the bear trap when it had somewhere nice like a greenhouse to sleep.

Ben wished he hadn't frightened it away. It would come back, wouldn't it? There were still sausage rolls in the fridge, although they might be a bit out of date. He hoped the bear wouldn't mind. He had a feeling bears weren't fussy about food, though. He raced back down the garden, almost tripping over the football, and hurled himself through the back door into the kitchen.

"What's the matter?" Dad asked, turning round from the oven. He was making tea. Ben chewed his lip. No way was Dad going to let him have sausage rolls if he was cooking tea already. He might just about stretch to an apple "if you're desperate" but Ben couldn't see the bear coming back for that. Besides, if it liked fruit and vegetables, it would have eaten the pumpkin, wouldn't it?

"Nothing... Just running." He looked meaningfully at Cassie, who was sitting at the kitchen table trying to learn her spellings. She was supposed to be covering up the list and then writing the words out, but she kept peering quickly under the magazine and then pretending to herself that she hadn't. She frowned back at him, making a *what?* face.

Ben rolled his eyes and gripped his stomach, miming being sick. Then he stared at her pleadingly.

Cassie folded her arms and glared at him. Then she held one hand out – how much would he pay?

"Go and get your hands washed for tea, Ben," Dad murmured. "It's nearly ready."

"A box of Smarties I've got hidden in our room," Ben whispered to her, and Cassie considered, and nodded.

"Dad!" she wailed. "Dad-deeee! I'm going to be sick!"

"Oh no…" Dad moaned, quickly turning the hob off and hurrying her towards the loo. "Really? Are you sure? Not again…" Cassie claimed to feel sick quite often. Ben was never sure quite how much she actually needed to be sick. But it was the perfect way to distract Dad.

Ben whipped the fridge door open and grabbed the sausage rolls, keeping half an eye on the kitchen door in case Dad came back. But Cassie was wailing in the downstairs loo, claiming that her stomach hurt and she was going to be really, really sick. She'd better not be too realistic or she wouldn't get tea, Ben thought as he slipped out of the back door.

As Ben raced past the bear trap he realized he didn't actually want to catch the bear. He just wanted to see it properly. But maybe he'd rather see it from their bedroom window. Just in case.

Most of all, he wanted to have a bear living in their greenhouse. No one else at school had a bear that slept under their pumpkin plants. Who cared about football when you had a pet bear? Ben scattered the sausage rolls carefully over the dirty floor of the greenhouse and stared hopefully at the pumpkin vines. But they didn't move.

The bear would come back, Ben told himself hopefully. Bears couldn't resist sausage rolls. Everyone knew that.

At bedtime, Ben wondered about asking Dad if he could camp in the back garden. He desperately wanted to see the bear again.

But it was probably too late for Dad to agree, seeing as they were already in bed. Plus if he camped out, Cassie would want to as well, and she'd told Dad earlier that she was feeling horribly sick and perhaps dying. Although she had then eaten enough spaghetti bolognese for a small army, so Dad hadn't been very convinced. He still wouldn't let her camp out all night though.

Of course, if the bear was really hungry, it might come and see if whatever was in the tent was edible. And what if it could tell the sausage rolls had gone off the day before? Ben's tent was made of very thin material. It definitely wouldn't keep out a bear, particularly one with a stomach ache from bad sausage rolls. Maybe watching from the garden shed would be better. It was just across the grass from the greenhouse, and it even had garden chairs in it. It would almost be cosy.

"You promised me Smarties," Cassie hissed at Ben as soon as Dad had finished reading to them and gone downstairs. "Dad wouldn't let me have any cake because I said I felt sick!"

"I know." Ben reached down the side of his bed and pulled the box out. "Here. You were brilliant. I needed to put more sausage rolls out for the bear. We should watch to see if he comes back."

"Comes *back*?" Ben could hear the sudden excitement in Cassie's voice. "You saw him too? Is that why you came running in like that?"

Ben shivered a little. Talking about bears in the half-dark of their room made him wonder if the garden was full of them already. "I think so. He was in the greenhouse. I saw his eyes. And his fur. He was a sort of golden-reddish colour."

"I told you! I told you!" Cassie squeaked. "You should have believed me."

"Mmm. Anyway, maybe you should save the Smarties. I think we'll need them for energy rations. To help us stay awake."

Cassie sighed. "I suppose so. But you have to give me all the orange ones." He heard her throw her duvet back, and she jumped out of bed and hurried to the window. "I can't see anything."

"That's why I'm going outside. To stake out the shed," Ben said, getting out of bed and putting his torch on so he could see where he'd left his fleecy jumper. "Coming?"

He flashed the torch at Cassie, and saw that she was gaping at him. He never did brave things like this. Ben knew it wasn't like him. But he was still going – he had to. He had to see the bear. Dave and Les had said that one day he would be famous – Les had even *paid* for one of his drawings. Ben had the Werther's Original hidden under his pillow still. Famous artists were always doing mad things.

Even so, Ben almost hoped that Dad would catch them, because then they wouldn't have to go and sit in a dark, spidery shed. But he also knew this was their best chance to see the bear for real.

Cassie grabbed her dressing gown, and after a moment's thought, she stuffed a small china bear into one of the pockets. Then she nodded at Ben, as if to say she was now fully equipped.

"Come on, then," Ben whispered, opening the bedroom and peering round it spy-fashion. Dad's door was closed. Good. The stairs were a bit creaky, but it was a noisy sort of house anyway – the pipes moaned, and there were odd pinging sounds from the radiators. They ought to be all right.

"I can't see where I'm putting my feet!" Cassie whispered, halfway down.

"Just feel!" Ben hissed back. "Or sit down and go on your bottom!"

The kitchen was eerie in the dark. The oven timer glowed, and Ben swallowed nervously as he crept over to the back door. He peered out through the window as he felt around for his wellies. The shed was down at the end of the garden, close to the trees, and it suddenly seemed a very long way away. He felt a small, chilly hand sneak into his as he turned the key and stepped out.

"What if the bear's in the garden already?" Cassie said worriedly. "We should have brought some food for it. It might eat us!"

That was exactly what Ben had been thinking, but he sniffed, "Of course it won't!" and having to be older-brotherly and brave gave him the confidence to march down the garden to the shed.

Ben knew he'd seen a couple of tatty garden chairs in the shed earlier on, and he hauled them out of the pile of stuff, setting them up just inside the door. Then they could sit with the door open a bit, and if the bear came close they could just shut it quickly. It couldn't be a really enormous bear or it wouldn't be able to get through the missing pane of glass in the greenhouse. So Ben was almost sure it wouldn't be big enough to pull the shed door open. Not if he and Cassie were both holding on to it.

They settled themselves in the chairs, peering round the door. The moon was out, and they could see the greenhouse quite clearly. Although with the moonlight reflecting off the glass they couldn't see inside properly – just the odd shadow of a leaf here and there.

"When will he come?" Cassie whispered.

"I don't know!" Ben sighed. He was beginning to wish he hadn't brought her. "Wait! Look! What's that?"

Cassie grabbed his arm as something shadowy lumbered down the garden. Ben could hear its heavy, thudding footsteps, and his own heartbeat seemed just as loud.

"Is it the bear?" Cassie whispered. "It doesn't look very furry…"

"I don't know…" The dark shape was so tall. It would definitely need to eat more than just a few sausage rolls. Ben reached out for the shed door, ready to slam it if the bear looked hungry.

"What are you two doing?" The lumbering shape was in front of the shed door now – it was Dad, in his dressing gown, and he looked very cross. "I thought you were in bed! I thought it was burglars trying to steal the lawnmower!"

Ben shone his torch at the lawnmower, which was very old, and had bits falling off it. "I don't think anyone would want our lawnmower, Dad," he said, his voice shaky with relief.

"Why aren't you in bed?" Dad snapped.

Ben considered trying to explain about the bear in the greenhouse, but Dad was already cross. It didn't seem like a good idea.

"We're looking for a bear," Cassie said brightly, and Ben groaned. He really shouldn't have brought her.

"My best bear. I left him in the shed, and I wanted him, and Ben said he'd help me find him." She held up the china bear from her pocket. "We found him, look!"

Dad sighed. "Next time, Cassie, love, ask me. Don't go out in the garden in the middle of the night."

7

"Want to play, Ben?"

Ben looked up cautiously from his sketchpad. He knew it was James standing there, with Kurt behind him, and all the other boys lined up behind them.

Somehow, even though James was smiling at him and his voice sounded friendly, Ben knew that it wasn't real. They were setting him up. They wanted him to jump up excitedly, and then they'd all laugh and tell him he couldn't play.

He folded his pad back over and rested both hands on it, gazing calmly up at James. Who cared about football? Famous artists with pet bears certainly didn't. Dave and Les were right. He should be proud of what he could do, instead of worrying about what he couldn't.

Ben rubbed the ball of his thumb over the cover of his sketchbook. He couldn't see the bear he'd been drawing, but he knew it was there. It wasn't done – it was only a pencil sketch, and he wasn't quite sure what colours he was going to use to finish it. When he'd seen the bear hurrying away from the greenhouse it had been shadowy under the trees, and he couldn't really be sure what colour it had been. Except that it hadn't been brown as he'd expected. More golden, or even red. He'd drawn it sitting among the pumpkin leaves, just parts of it showing, here and there.

He might give it red paws and a red muzzle, to stand out against the green leaves.

"Do you want to play?" James snapped, sounding quite a lot less friendly. Clearly he'd expected Ben to leap at the chance. His big show-off moment wasn't going the way he'd thought it would.

Ben smiled at him. "No."

James looked comically surprised. His mouth almost fell open. "What?" he demanded. "Why not?"

"I'm not bothered about football." Ben shrugged. "I'm busy."

James recovered himself. "Busy doing what?" he demanded scornfully. "Drawing some stupid *picture*?" He turned round to look at the others. "Ahhh, Ben's colouring!"

Obediently, they sniggered. But they were looking bored, and Kurt was tapping the ball back and forth between his feet.

Sam darted a guilty, unhappy look at Ben, as though he was sorry. "Come on, James. We want to get on with the game. Break's going to be finished soon."

"We wouldn't let you join in anyway," James told Ben crossly. "You're useless. Isn't he?" he snarled, turning back to the others. But somehow his glory had worn off a little, and they only shrugged and muttered, which made James even crosser. He leaned closer to Ben. "I'd rather have your little sister play than you," he spat. "At least she could probably kick the ball the right way."

Ben pressed his fingers harder on to the

sketchbook and thought about the bear lurking inside. And about how brave he'd been the night before, looking for it out in the dark. He smiled wider at James, showing his teeth like a bear. "Yeah, but I don't think my little sister would want to play with you," he said, shaking his head. "She thinks you're a bit useless."

James gaped at him in a fishy sort of way, and the other boys grinned – at Ben – and wandered off to start their game, leaving James to follow after them, shouting orders. They didn't seem to be listening to him all that much.

Ben let out a shaky breath and opened his sketchbook again, looking down at his bear. "Thanks," he whispered.

He didn't want to finish the sketch in the playground – it was too important. He'd wait till he was home. Maybe even until he'd seen the bear again. He'd nipped out to the greenhouse this morning before breakfast, and the sausage rolls had been gone, but there had been no sign of the bear. Ben hadn't searched under the leaves – they were the bear's bed, and it seemed too rude. Instead, he'd left a small pile of honey-roasted peanuts, and an egg. It was an odd breakfast, but he hadn't had a lot of time to look in the cupboards – only a few minutes while Dad was shaving.

Ben turned over another page in his sketchbook and looked thoughtfully at the boys kicking the ball around on the other side of the playground. Then he started to draw, smiling and humming to himself a little. Bears were much cooler than football – but he'd never thought of putting the two together...

Ben sketched in a football pitch, with goals, and two teams of chunky-looking bears. Then he laughed and added the final bear – the one who actually had the ball, which was stuck on his claws, and completely flat. The bear looked a bit confused and Ben quickly changed all the rest of his team too, so that they were rolling their eyes at him.

"That's really funny!"

Ben looked up in surprise. He'd been enjoying himself so much, he hadn't realized he'd got an audience.

Joe, one of the boys from his class who'd been in the football game, was sitting near him on the wall.

"I thought you were playing with James and Kurt and that lot," Ben said, looking vaguely across the playground.

"Gave up. James is having some stupid argument with Sam. And it's his ball. Got bored waiting. You should do a football comic. You're really good."

"I don't know that much about football," Ben said, shrugging.

"Mmmm. Maybe." Joe looked embarrassed. "You shouldn't listen to James, you know. He's a pain."

Ben stared at him. "But…"

Joe sighed. "I know. He's good at bossing everyone around. And no one wants to get on the wrong side of him." He looked hopefully, shyly at Ben. "Could you do a picture of me? Please? I'll sit still."

Ben nodded. "OK. It might not be any good… Oh – James is yelling at you. I think they're starting again." He waited for Joe to leap up, but he didn't – he moved closer to Ben and looked at him eagerly.

"Doesn't matter. I can play football any time."

Ben tore the Sellotape off with his teeth, and carefully stuck the page to the glass. He was putting it in the corner, behind some of the leaves, so that Dad wouldn't notice. The bear might not notice either, but Ben loved thinking that he might see his artwork. Everyone else had liked it. Joe had told lots of the others in his class, and people kept coming and asking Ben if they could see it. He'd talked to more people that day than he had in weeks. And loads of people had asked him to draw their portraits. He was going to be busy every lunch time.

He smoothed the paper admiringly and let himself out of the greenhouse with a last, hopeful look at the pumpkin plants, watching for a glint of reddish fur. Then he hurried back into the house – the new staircase up to the loft was in place, and Dave and Les had promised that he could have his first proper look at his new room today.

Until now they'd been getting up to it with the scaffolding and with ladders, and Ben had only been able to peer up through the ceiling. But now he would actually be able to walk up on his very own stairs. Ben loved stairs. He was intending to use them as a bookcase as well. And Dad said he could have hooks all up the wall for hanging his drawings. Feeling excited, he flung himself up the stairs to the first floor, and practically ran into Dave and Les and Dad, who were standing at the bottom of the new staircase, eyeing the banisters thoughtfully and talking about paint.

Dave grinned at him. "Aha. Come to see it, have you? It'll look strange, though – the walls still need plastering. Just don't be disappointed."

Ben shook his head. "I won't." He sniffed happily – the stairs smelled of wood, a fresh, spicy sort of smell. And he loved the way they curled round, leading up into his room. He couldn't believe this was all his. "Are you sure, Dad?" he asked suddenly. "You're sure I can have this room? You don't want it?"

Dad shook his head. "Nope. I'd keep worrying I was going to walk into the roof."

Ben nodded. Dad had explained that the loft room would have sloping ceilings to fit into the roof space. It was tall enough to stand up in the middle, but sloped down at the sides.

But then Dad was over six foot – it didn't worry Ben.

"Go on then!" Dad said, giving him a gentle push.

Ben walked slowly up the stairs, finding it hard to believe that they hadn't been there this morning when he'd left for school. They creaked gently underneath him, and he peered hopefully up towards his room.

Parts of the walls and ceiling were still covered in silvery stuff, which Dad had told him was to keep the heat in. The proper walls and the paint would go over the top. But he could see what the room would be like in the end.

"It's huge," Ben whispered.

"Do you like it?" Dad asked anxiously, coming up the stairs behind him.

"It's brilliant. I can't believe how big it is."

"I'll show you the best bit," Les said. He crouched down at the side of the room, where it was lowest. "You've got a secret compartment. There's a little door here, do you see? Leads into the roof space. Put a chair in front of that, and you've got a cupboard nobody knows about."

Ben nodded. "Or my bean bag... It's like the secret compartment in your toolbox."

Les blinked. "How did you know about that?"

Ben looked apologetic. "Cassie saw it. She said there's an extra little bit inside that you never open. She thinks it's got emeralds and diamonds in it."

Les sucked his teeth and eyed Ben thoughtfully. "Want to see what's really in it?"

Ben's eyes widened. "Yes! Please, I mean."

Les chuckled. "You might not think it's that exciting. Better let Cassie go on believing it's treasure." He flipped a catch and opened the little box up, pulling out a paper bag, which he offered to Ben. It was full of round, dark reddish things. Ben looked at them, trying to work out what they were. Not any sort of treasure, he was pretty sure. He sniffed, and the strong, sweet smell reminded him of Grandpa, who lived on the other side of town.

"Aniseed balls!" he said, giggling. "You've got aniseed balls hidden in your toolbox?"

"I love aniseed balls. They make very good treasure, and I have to keep them hidden; Dave would nick them all otherwise." Les grinned at him. "Right. I need to go and get started on filling in the soakaway – your bear trap, I mean."

"Filling it in?" Ben frowned. "Why?"

"Ah, well, we've decided your bears are friendly. We don't want to catch them. And…" Les paused, and looked at Ben sideways. "We're finishing off now. Bit more plastering, and the painting. We should have filled the bear trap in ages ago, to be honest, but then the new materials for up here arrived, and we wanted to get on…"

Ben stared at him. "So – so you'll be going? You're going soon?"

Les looked around the room thoughtfully. "Another week? Maybe week and a half?"

Ben gulped. Of course they had to go sometime. He'd known that they would. And he wanted his new room to be finished. But he hadn't thought it would be quite so soon. He hadn't realized quite how much he would miss them, either. No one else believed he was going to be a famous artist. No one else had wanted to buy one of his drawings. It was going to be a lot harder to be brave without Dave and Les.

8

"They're going?" Cassie wailed. "They can't! I need them!"

Ben nodded, gulping. "So do I."

Cassie stood up from in front of the game of bear school she'd been playing and folded her arms stubbornly. "I'm going to make them stay."

Ben shook his head miserably. "You can't, Cass. They're builders. They have to go when they've finished the work. They – they'll go to someone else's house."

Cassie stared at him, round-eyed. "And talk to other children instead?"

"I suppose so." Ben shrugged. "Or there might not be children at all."

Cassie scowled. "What a waste." It was one of Dad's favourite comments, usually about leftover cereal.

"Where are you going?" Ben asked as she stalked to the bedroom door. She was walking funny, lifting her feet up and stepping on tiptoes. It was her secretive walk, the one she did for being a spy, or a detective.

"Wait and see. I'll be back in a minute." Cassie vanished along the landing, and Ben lay down on his bed, put his chin in his hands and sighed. Just when everything had been going so well. School had been all right again today, but that had been because of the bear, and his drawing. What if it all stopped working when

Dave and Les weren't there to tell him he was an artist?

Ben had a horrible feeling that everything would be the way it was before, and the bear's page in his book would be like James had said – just colouring.

Cassie had crept back downstairs with a bag of screws, a hammer and a large tin of paint. She hid them under her bed. Her plan was to keep stealing things until Les and Dave ran out of tools and couldn't finish the loft room.

Ben wasn't convinced this was going to work – the builders had about six hammers each, he'd seen them. And they were always putting them down and leaving them in places.

They probably wouldn't even notice that any were gone.

By the next afternoon, Cassie had started to agree with him. The space under her bed was full, and Dave and Les hadn't mentioned that any tools were missing. She'd even got a cordless drill under there.

Ben was curled silently into the corner of his bed, not drawing, or making Lego. He didn't feel like it.

The front doorbell rang, and Cassie jumped up, hurtling down the stairs to get there first.

Ben wondered vaguely who it was. Cassie seemed to be arguing with them, and now Dad was hurrying down the stairs to join in.

At last the front door slammed shut, and Cassie raced into their room and banged their door shut too.

Ben sat up worriedly. He could hear Dad thumping up the stairs after her. "What did you do? Why's Dad cross?"

Cassie sat on the edge of her bed, her arms folded and a stubborn look on her face. "I told the man with the new floorboards to go away. That he'd got the wrong house."

Ben stared at her. "Why?"

"So Dave and Les couldn't finish, of course, stupid!"

"What on earth were you doing?" Dad shouted as he shoved the door open. "I've just had to apologize to the poor man! I had to practically beg him to let us keep those boards. What sort of silly, irresponsible game was that, Cassie?"

Cassie looked at him, and sniffed, and let a

couple of tears run down her cheeks. She was a very clever crier, but Ben thought she actually meant it this time.

"Don't do that." Dad sighed. "Look, you must have had a reason."

There was a tiny silence, and then Cassie whispered, "We don't want them to go."

"Who? The builders?" Dad crouched down in front of her. "Why not? You want this to be your own bedroom, don't you?" He frowned. "Are you worried about not having Ben to share with any more? Will you be lonely?"

Cassie shook her head. "Course not. I'll have my bears." She gulped. "But we need Dave and Les. They talk to us. They tell us pirate stories, and then Ben draws them. And they look at Ben's pictures. You don't."

Dad's face seemed to sag a little. He turned round to look at Ben. "I look at them," he said, rather quietly.

Ben shrugged. "You've been really busy…"

"Ben thinks those boys at school will be horrible to him again," Cassie called from half under her bed, where she was pulling out screwdrivers, and a hammer drill, and a pile of paintbrushes. "Do you know, I don't think Dave and Les even noticed I took all these."

"What boys?" Dad rubbed his hands over his head, stretching his eyebrows up in the way he did when he was worried. "What's been happening? Ben, you never said about any of this!"

"I tried…" Ben muttered. "I asked you

about football. You said I was useless, just like everybody at school does."

"I didn't!" Dad sounded horrified. "I'd never say that!"

"You said I'd never be any good at football, and I should just stick to running." Ben hunched his shoulders, not looking at Dad, but Dad crouched down in front of him and put a hand on his knee. "Ben, I'm really sorry. I can't have been listening properly. I never wanted to upset you. I just meant..."

"It's all right, Dad," Ben said dully. "I know I'm useless. I don't care. I don't want to play any more, so it doesn't matter."

"You're much better at drawing anyway," Cassie told him loyally. "Claudia wants you to draw her too, please. In a pirate dress, like mine, but you have to make hers not as nice. But I told her she'd have to queue up till next week, at least. Everyone wants Ben to draw them, Dad. He's famous."

"I won't be any more. Not when the builders go." Ben turned and stared hopelessly out of the window. "They were the ones who said I was good."

Cassie shook her head. "No. All my friends say you're famous now, Ben. And the bear's still there. You'll still be able to draw him."

Ben shrugged, and glanced out into the garden again. "Maybe." He knew the bear had been there before Dave and Les came, but he couldn't help thinking that they were the ones who'd made him see. What if the bear never came back?

"What bear? What are you two talking about?" Dad said, looking confused.

"Look, come and see. Come on, Ben." Cassie grabbed his hands and tried to pull. "Show him."

"Please, Ben," Dad agreed, putting a hand on his shoulder. "I won't ever know what's going on if you don't tell me."

"You're supposed to *see!*" Ben said suddenly. "You weren't ever looking! I shouldn't need to tell you!"

Dad swallowed, and then nodded slowly. "You're right. And I am sorry. But please can you tell me now?"

Ben got up and followed them downstairs. He wasn't sure if he wanted Dad to see the picture stuck up on the greenhouse glass. Dad was fussy about the greenhouse; he always said it wasn't for playing in. "You don't have to come and see," he said suddenly, halfway down the stairs, looking panicked. "It doesn't matter. Forget it."

Dad looked up at him, shaking his head. "Yes, it does matter." His face was hurt, and Ben didn't want to be the one making him look like that.

"All right!" he said hurriedly, jumping a couple of steps. "But don't be cross."

Dad shook his head, and they walked out into the garden, Cassie pulling Dad by the hand and Dad with his arm round Ben's shoulders, until they came to the greenhouse.

Cassie shoved the door open and peered in cautiously. "He isn't here," she called back to Ben.

"What if he followed Dave and Les?" Ben gulped.

"No. I don't think he'll go just because they do." Cassie shook her head. "He was always here, wasn't he? They only told us about him."

"Who was?" Dad asked, sounding bewildered.

Ben leaned over and pulled back the leaves so Dad could see the picture. "There's a bear that lives in here. Like one of these bears. Seeing him gave me the idea to draw this, and loads of people at school liked it. No one's ever liked my drawings before. I fed him all those sausage rolls that were in the fridge," he added. "Sorry."

"It's a brilliant drawing." Dad went closer, admiring the football strips, and the way the ball was stuck on the striker's claws. "It's really funny too. You're getting so good. But – a bear?" Dad looked at them doubtfully.

"Yes." Cassie nodded firmly. "An orangey one. Not too big. It comes in through this hole, look." She lifted the leaves so Dad could see the big missing pane of glass.

Dad leaned over, staring out of the hole, and then he looked at Ben. "I'm glad I didn't get a new sheet of glass, then. Does the bear sleep on that compost bag? Would I ever see him, do you think?"

Ben breathed in sharply, some of the tight feeling inside him easing away. "You might," he agreed cautiously. "Maybe. If you were lucky."

9

"You'll see us again, you know." Les stroked Cassie's hair and leaned over to try to look at her, but she had her face buried in his fleece.

"We won't!" Cassie wailed, her voice muffled. "You're not coming back. Dad said so. Everything's finished."

"We'll come back if anything goes wrong," Dave explained. "Which isn't to say you're to go round hitting things with that hammer you nicked off me, Cassie."

"We'll be coming back to fetch all the tools you've got hidden all over the place," Les said, shaking his head. "I'll be on another job, looking for my best screwdriver, and it'll be hidden in your airing cupboard."

Cassie looked up, shaking her curls out of her eyes. Her face was red, and sticky with tears. "I gave them back! All of them, I really did."

"The airing cupboard?" Dad looked worried. "I didn't know you had them in there as well."

"It's all right." Dave nudged him. "We saw her doing it," he said quietly. "We got them all out again."

"But I didn't just mean you'd see us here, anyway," Les explained. "I moor up along the canal, here and there. You'll see me going past. And Dave comes along for a ride on the boat every so often. You get your dad to bring you down past the canal for a walk now and then. If you see *Midnight*, you can come and have a cup of tea with us. And an aniseed ball," he added, grinning at Ben. "Actually, I've got something for you." He handed Ben a small white paper bag. "To go in your secret cupboard," he whispered. "You can eat them while you're drawing. And some rhubarb and custards for you, Cassie."

"Thanks," Ben whispered, but Cassie only sniffed.

"Keep an eye out for the bear too," Dave put in. "He's good luck, that bear."

Ben nodded, his hand wrapped tightly in Dad's. Dad hadn't seen the bear yet, but Ben knew he wanted to, which was what mattered. "Bye," he said. "We'll watch out for you on the canal. We'll see you."

Dave and Les waved as they got into the truck, and then they drove away, the cement mixer wobbling a bit in the back.

Cassie trailed back inside, and Ben looked down the empty street, feeling flat.

"You could draw…" Dad suggested hesitantly. "Something about them going. You could even give it to them. We could post it to Dave. Or wait till we saw Les on his boat."

Ben nodded, wondering what he might draw. A pirate ship sailing away, maybe? With him and Cassie marooned on a desert island? He smiled to himself. With a bear balanced in the top of a palm tree, all worried and wobbly.

"Dad, will you come and chat to me while I draw?" he asked hopefully. "Can we have hot chocolate? I bet that's what would make Cassie feel better."

Cassie suddenly appeared in the doorway. "With marshmallows."

Dad nodded, leading Ben inside. "Mm-hm. And I've got an idea. You go and start your drawing, and I'll show you."

Ben lay on the top of his new cabin bed, colouring the dark sea in ripples. The pirate ship looked black and sad, but somehow the Ben and Cassie on the island didn't seem too miserable being left behind. The bear looked as though it was going to fall out of the palm tree any minute, though.

"Hot chocolate," Dad said, coming carefully up the stairs with a tray. "Well. Some. There's six marshmallows in it, so I don't think there's room for much actual chocolate. Cassie said six was the right number."

Cassie was watching Ben smugly through the steam wisping off her mug. Marshmallows were her favourite.

"What was your idea?" Ben asked, slurping carefully on a bit of hot marshmallow.

"Bear-watching." Dad craned his neck to peer out of the long window in Ben's sloping ceiling. "You said when you saw him before it was late afternoon, just as it was starting to get dark. It's about that time now. And I reckon, if we all sit on top of your bed, we can see the trees and the greenhouse out of this window. Maybe we'll see him coming across the garden." He glanced sideways at Ben. "I did leave him a cold sausage left over from last night's tea. I put it down for him when I watered the pumpkins."

Ben nodded, smiling. "It's just the right time," he agreed. "But you have to promise not to spill hot chocolate on my bed," he told Cassie warningly as she started up his bunkbed ladder, and she rolled her eyes and sniffed at him. But she was careful as she settled down at the end of the bed.

They sipped the chocolate, admiring Ben's drawing, and watching the shadows pool together across the garden as it grew darker.

"I don't think he's coming," Cassie said crossly. "Can we watch TV?"

"I suppose so." Dad sighed. But Ben gripped his hand.

"Look," he whispered. "Cassie, by the fence!"

They leaned forward, watching a dark
shadow lumbering across the garden, weaving
in and out of the shadows of the trees, until it
slipped behind the greenhouse.

"He's gone to eat that sausage," Ben said,
leaning against Dad's arm.

Dad nodded. "Good thing I left him something." He wrapped his arm round Ben, and then stretched. "I suppose I should go and cook some dinner. What are you going to do?"

"Finish my drawing," Ben told him, pulling the tin of pencils out from under his pillow. "I hadn't got the bear quite right. But I can see where I went wrong now. I really want to finish it."

Dad nodded as he angled his long legs down the ladder and lifted Cassie down after him.

"Keep watching. And keep drawing. We want to see too."

If you liked
LOOKING for Bear,
try this!

Everyone thinks Penguin is a silly name for
a cat, but Alfie thinks it's perfect. To Alfie,
he's the best cat in the world.

Penguin loves to play in the overgrown garden
next door. But when a new girl moves in and
reclaims it, Alfie worries she might think
Penguin belongs to her too!

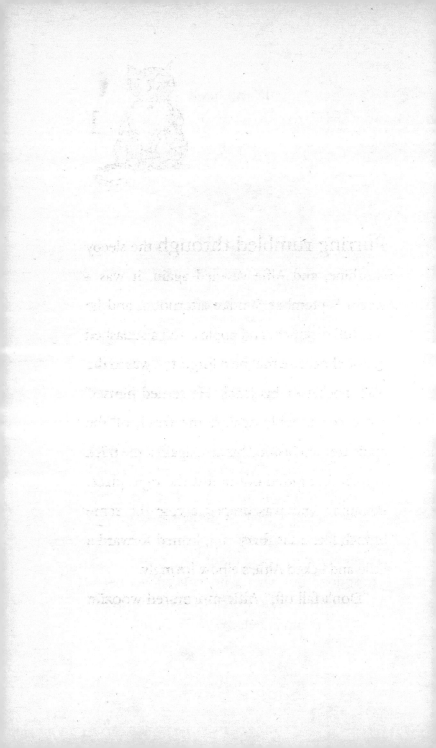

1

Purring rumbled through the sleepy sunshine, and Alfie yawned again. It was a warm September Sunday afternoon, and he was full of lunch, and apples, and a squashed bar of chocolate that he'd forgotten was in the back pocket of his jeans. He settled himself more comfortably against the trunk of the apple tree and leaned his arm against the thick branch that jutted out in just the right place. Penguin, who was draped across the same branch like a fat furry rug, leaned forward a little and licked Alfie's elbow lovingly.

"Don't fall off," Alfie murmured woozily.

But it was a silly thing to say. Penguin never fell. He didn't look as though he was in the best shape for climbing trees – one would think his stomach would get in the way, particularly for jumping. But Penguin had perfect balance, good even for a cat. Alfie smiled to himself as he remembered trying to persuade Penguin to walk along the washing line during the summer holidays. Penguin had refused, even for smoky bacon crisps, his favourite. (Although he had stolen the crisps off the table later.) Alfie had been convinced that Penguin would be a fabulous tightrope artist. They should try again. Perhaps it was the lack of circus music and Big Top atmosphere that had put him off. Maybe a costume... Alfie looked at Penguin thoughtfully. He wondered how easy it would be to get hold of a cat-shaped leotard.

Penguin opened one yellowish-golden eye a slit and stared sternly at Alfie, as though warning him that attempts to dress him in a sequinned cloak would result in severe scratches. But he didn't stop purring.

"OK," Alfie murmured. "But I bet it would be good for your tummy."

Penguin ignored that. He didn't have any problems with the size of his stomach.

Penguin hadn't always been enormous. When Alfie had first found him, sitting on the front doorstep on the way home from school two years before, he had been very skinny indeed, and not much more than a kitten. Alfie was pretty sure he'd been a stray for a while, and that was why he loved food so much – he'd never been quite sure where the next meal was coming from.

Mum and Dad hadn't been at all sure about keeping the thin little black and white kitten, but Alfie had begged and begged. He had agreed to putting up posters, just in case someone else was looking for their lost cat, and he'd stood anxiously next to Mum as she had phoned all the vets in the local phonebook. But no one had turned up to claim the skinny kitten (who was already less skinny, after a couple of days of Alfie-sized meals). After two weeks, Mum and Dad had given in, and Alfie had announced the secret he'd been saving up.

The cat was called Penguin.

Dad had tried to explain that it was ridiculous to call a cat that. He *wasn't* a penguin.

Alfie said he knew that quite well, thank you. The cat just looked like one. And it was true. Penguin had sleek black fur – getting sleeker by the day – and a shining white shirt front. When Alfie had spent his birthday money from Gran on a glow-in-the-dark orange collar, Penguin was a dead ringer for his namesake. When Alfie phoned Gran to tell her what he'd spent the money on, he had got a little parcel back with a silvery tag engraved with his phone number on one side and *Penguin* on the other. Gran liked cats. And even Dad could not argue now there was a collar with his name on.

Alfie sometimes wondered what would have happened if Penguin had chosen someone else's step to sit on that day. Where would he be now? It was impossible to imagine not having him there. Penguin was his best friend. Alfie had lots of friends at school, but he never talked to them as much as he talked to Penguin. Penguin was an excellent listener, and he always purred in all the right places. Once, when Alfie was telling him about being kept in at lunch time by Mrs Haynes, the Year Two teacher he had never got on with, Penguin had coughed up a hairball all over the kitchen floor. Which just proved that he understood exactly what Alfie had been talking about.

Alfie liked Penguin plump. He thought it made him look even more penguin-like. But at his last check-up, the vet had suggested politely that Penguin ought to go on a diet, and Mum had bought a bag of special diet cat food. It did not look pleasant. Alfie hated the smell of the tins Penguin usually had, and forked it quickly into his bowl with his nose stuffed in the crook of his elbow. But at least the tinned stuff was meaty. Like something a proper cat might want to eat, after a hard day's prowling around after mice and birds. The diet version looked like rabbit poo.

Alfie had tried to explain to Mum that it wasn't going to work, but she hadn't been in a very good mood, as his baby sister Jess had just thrown a bowlful of lovingly mashed carrots into the toaster.

"If he doesn't like it, he won't eat it," she'd snapped, trying to fish the orange goo out with a spoon. "And that'll have the same effect in the long run. Stop fussing, Alfie!"

Alfie had sighed, and measured the correct, tiny amount of diet food into Penguin's bowl. It didn't even cover the fish pattern on the bottom. Alfie had crossed his fingers behind his back and set it down in front of Penguin, who was coiling himself adoringly around Alfie's ankles.

Penguin had stopped dead, and stared up at Alfie accusingly.

"Sorry! The vet said!" Alfie protested. "Your legs are going to start hurting if you don't go on a diet."

Penguin sniffed suspiciously at the little brown pellets, then turned round and went straight out of the cat flap.

Later that evening, two sausages mysteriously disappeared while Alfie's mum wasn't looking.

The diet cat food lasted about a week before Mum binned it. She told Alfie that it was expensive anyway, but since she'd now had to replace most of what was in the fridge as well, it was like feeding three cats instead of one.

Penguin sat on one of the kitchen chairs looking happily plump and watched as she put the rest of the bag into the bin.

"That cat is smirking at me!" Mum said

crossly, as she clanged the bin shut. "This really can't go on, Alfie. It's for his own good!"

"I don't think he thinks he's fat," Alfie explained.

"You'll just have to make sure he gets more exercise." Mum sniffed. "Maybe you should put a sausage on a string and make him chase it up and down the garden."

Now, looking at Penguin's stomach gently folding over the edges of the branch, Alfie had to admit he was larger than he should be. But it was hard to make a cat exercise when he didn't want to. Alfie had tried racing up and down the garden, and even throwing a bouncy ball for Penguin to chase. Penguin had sat on the garden bench, eyeing him with fascinated interest, as though he wondered why Alfie was bothering. After all, it wasn't as if he was a dog.

Look out for more by
HOLLY WEBB

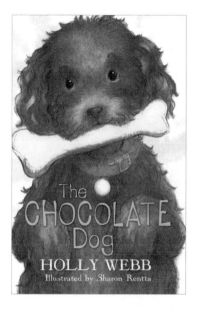

Amy already has one naughty little sister, so why do her parents need another baby? Will there be any room left for Amy?

At least she has her dog, Choc. He makes Amy feel like she's the most important person in the world. But can Choc help Amy see that she's special to her family, too?

HOLLY has always loved animals. As a child, she had two dogs, a cat, and at one point, nine gerbils (an accident). Holly's other love is books. Holly now lives in Reading with her husband, three sons and a very spoilt cat.